The Christmas Book of Hope

written by

Jeff Verney

illustrated by

Frederick H. Carlson

JRV Publishing   West Simsbury   Connecticut

copyright ©2006 Jeff Verney
art ©2006 Frederick H. Carlson

First Edition
Library of Congress Cataloging-in-Publication Data
Library of Congress Control Number: 2005909041

Verney, Jeff
        The Christmas Book of Hope/by Jeff Verney.-1st ed.
        Summary: A long lost faith-filled book written by one of Santa's elves brings hope to a boy in his time of need.
        ISBN 0-9771250-0-9

Printed in Hong Kong

The illustrations for this book were done in graphite, watercolor, and gouache on Strathmore board.
The type is Garamond for text, and headers were set in Apple Chancery.

To Sam and Pam, who bring love, laughter, and light to every single day.
J.R.V.

To my supporting family (Nancy, Ellen and Rick),
and to the faithful parishioners of St. Alban's Episcopal Church/Murrysville, PA,
and to the Lord during this and every Christmas season...
F.H.C.

The Winter of 1706
was harsh, and little
Timothy Smith
was in the
worst of ways.

His parents were sick,
there was hardly
any food, and
no joy was found in
Timothy's house
as Christmas
drew near.

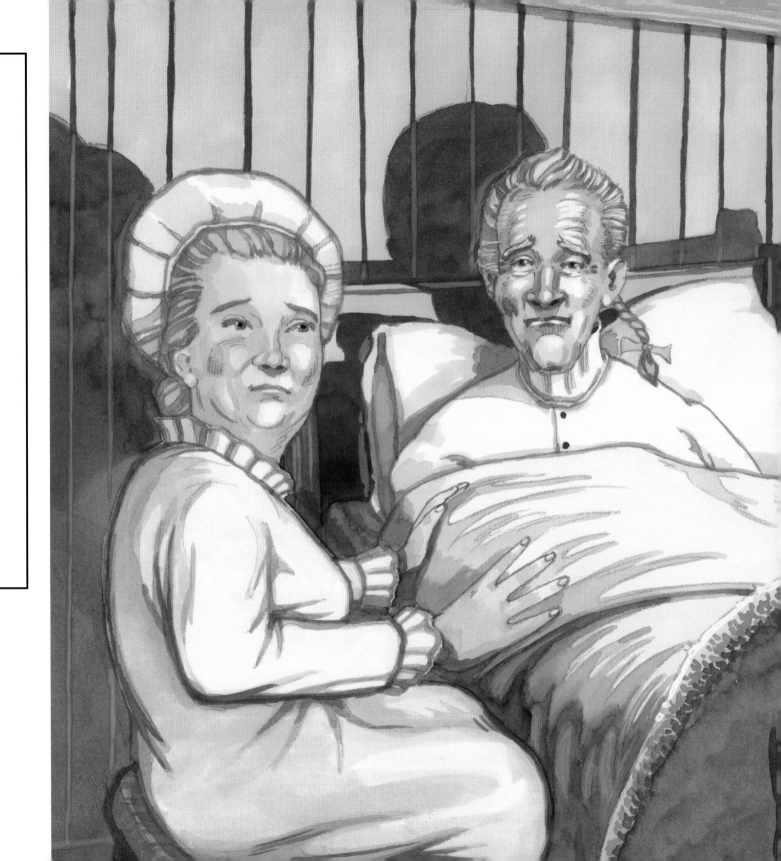

Every night he would pray to Jesus for help, but things seemed so hopeless to Timothy.

Timothy wrote his
Christmas letter
and sent it to Santa,
and when
Santa read the letter,
he frowned
and called for Sol,
the eldest, wisest elf.

"This poor little boy
and his family are
suffering so much,"
said Santa.

"We need to give
them a gift that will
help them believe that
things will get better."

Sol thoughtfully stroked his beard and after thinking for a few moments replied, "I know. A book!"

"A book of hope.
A reminder of why we
celebrate Christmas."

He smiled and
continued,
"I'll go write it."

On Christmas Eve,
the elves were putting
the last of the gifts
into Santa's bag.

Sol rushed in
and said,
"I've finished the book
for Timothy Smith!"
placing the book
on the very top
of Santa's bag.

But when the elves
carried the bag to
Santa's sleigh,
no one saw the book
slide off the bag
and under one of
Santa's workbenches.

Later that evening, Santa came down the chimney into Timothy's house, and sitting by the fire were Timothy and his parents.

"Oh Santa!"
cried Timothy,
"My parents are
getting better!"

"I think Jesus
heard my prayers!"

"Ho! Ho! Ho! That's wonderful!" exclaimed Santa, but when he looked into his bag for Timothy's gift, he could not find it.

"That's all right,"
said Timothy.

"Having my parents
get healthy is
the best gift of all!
Merry Christmas!"

For many years
Santa wondered
what had happened to
Timothy's gift,
but as the centuries
passed, the book,
which gathered
much dust under
Santa's workbench,
was slowly forgotten.

Until three hundred
years later.

"This letter just breaks my heart," sighed Santa to Sol.

"It seems like everything that can go wrong has happened to Timmy Smith.

And he's such a good boy. If there was only a gift that would let him see that things can be better."

"Timmy Smith," mused Sol.

"Timmy...Timmy... Timothy Smith! Remember that book I wrote for Timothy Smith so many years ago? The one that was lost?"

He looked at Santa
with a sad look
in his eyes.

"I suppose I could
try writing
another book.
But that one
was so perfect.
If only we knew
where it was."

Three elves burst into Santa's office, carrying a very old dusty book.

"Santa! Santa!
Look what
we found!"

"It was underneath
one of the old
workbenches!"

Santa blew the dust
off of the book
and looked at Sol
with a twinkle
in his eyes.

"I guess you won't
have to rewrite
the book after all."

"Looks like we have our own Christmas miracle tonight."

"We'll make sure it doesn't get lost this year!"

On Christmas morning after saying his prayers, Timmy Smith trudged downstairs, not expecting to find anything under the sparsely decorated Christmas tree.

Waiting for him was a book with a note from Santa.

The note read:
"Dear Timmy,
I meant to give
this book to
one of your ancestors
hundreds of years
ago, but it got lost
before I delivered it."

"I think the reason the
book disappeared
was that it was
meant for you."

"Merry Christmas!
-Santa Claus"

Timmy sat down
by the fireplace
and opened the book,
which was called
*The Christmas Book
of Hope*.

He read about all
of the blessings
life can bring.

He read about
the power of prayer
and the
magic of faith.

Most importantly,
he read that if
you believe in Jesus,
God will take
care of you,
especially when
times are bad.

Timmy shut the book
and said a prayer
of thanks to Santa
and to Jesus.

"Merry Christmas,
Santa!" he exclaimed,
looking up
the fireplace.

"Happy Birthday,
Jesus!" he proclaimed,
looking out
a window up
towards the heavens.

And for
the first time in
a long time
Timmy Smith
smiled, knowing
that things
would get better
because he
truly believed.

The End.